The Cosmic Element

Flairs and Glairs
Publication House

"The Cosmic Element"

ISBN No: " 9789391302412"
1st Edition
Language – English and Hindi

Flairs and Glairs
Publication House
Regd. Under MSME Act.

Disclaimer

This is a work of fiction and solely represent the thoughts of the corresponding authors of the articles. Our editors have tried their best to edit the content of all the authors and check the plagiarism.

All the write-ups in this book are unique and are only published in this book.

In case any plagiarism or error is found, only the author is responsible alone, and not the publisher or the Compilers.

Cover Designing and Book Formatting
Shubham Shah and Ishani Agarwal

Acknowledgment

Dear Almighty, thank you for blessing me with the power and zeal to be able to complete this Anthology.

Also, Thank You dear parents, for trusting in me, and letting me work whenever I wanted. My family is the one who supported me for what I am today.

When it comes to this, Anthology, I would like to start with Thanking the Co -Authors, without your help and support, I would have never been able to complete it.

Thank you all of you, for being there. Much Love to all of you. I am glad to see you all standing by me.

Co Author

Shubham Shah (Founder Flairs and Glairs)
Ishani Agarwal (Co Founder Flairs and Glairs)
Shivangi Jaiswal (Compiler)

1.Dushyant Walia
2.Shivansh Sharma
3.Raj jot
4.Vaishnavi Hend
5.Sahina Ghugha
6.राशिका
7.Sneha Ahuja
8.Aishwarya Umashankar
9.Kalamkaar
10.Shruti Dash
11.Shradha Gindlani
12.Rushda
13.Ravi Ahirwar
14.Vikash Kumar Bhakat
15.Riya Srivastava
16.Ashwini Singh
17.Muskan Sachdeva
18.Abhilash Sharma
19.Anwesa Chakraborty
20.Sonal Saha
21.Ami Patel
22.Dipti David
23.Kehinde Margret Makinde

24.Payal Indani
25.M.Haseebunissa
26.Gurdeep Kaur
27.Priya Srivastava
28.Sushmita Ray Choudhury
29.Neeti Yadav
30.Shivani Priyanga
31.Komal Singh
32.Reshma Sultana
33.Avneet Kaur
34.Ashis Pahi
35.Priyanshi Mittal
36.Vishal K R
37.T. Priyadharshini
38.Aditi Kumari
39.Navjot Singh
40.Maniska Das
41.Mohanapriya.K
42.Husaina S
43.Adhyatm Singh
44.Poojalakshmi. V
45.Rupsha Mitra

Shubham Shah

(Founder- Flairs and Glairs)

Shubham Shah, an entrepreneur at "Flairs & Glairs" a brand with dynamics in events organizing and cultural educational pan INDIA, is a 26yrs old guy who recently has entered the digital platform of imprinting emotions. He has initiated with his own open mic platform to help budding poets and aspiring writers under his brand named as "Teekhe Zasbaaat"

He is a commerce graduate from the Bhagalpur City of Bihar. He states Writing has impersonated him since childhood and he has now been writing for over a decade!
Cooking, on the other hand, is his passion! He also mentions, trying out new things just tickles him!
When asked sir, Why SPICY EMOTIONS?
He smiled and added, "agar jasbaat teekhe na ho toh wo jasbaat kahan" Spices are all that blends! So do his words!
As a chef, he presents to you his dish! Hot and freshly served! Taste it! Feel it! Enjoy it! You can also find his writing in the Book "Teekhe Zasbaaat" and 50+ Co -authored anthologies.
With his passion to explore opportunities across Platforms, he is working with keen dev otion and We wish him all the very best for his future ventures.
He is Featured in the International Magazine DeMode for his upcoming solo novel.
He is Approved by Ne8x for its Lit Fest, and is a Golden Star Awards 2020 Winner.
He is a India Book of Records Holder for his Anthology Satrang, and has the Grandmaster title by Asia Book of Records, for the same.
He has also been featured in Prabhat Khabar, Dainik Jagran, and a lot of other Newspapers in Bihar for his achievements.
He has been a proud co-author to
India Book Of Records (Title- Black)
World Book Of Records (Title -15 Wonders of Poetries)
India Book Of Records (Title - Aaina)
Vajra World Records Holder (Title - Gustakhi Maaf Hai)
High Range of Records Holder (Title - Gustakhi Maaf Hai)
Indian Book of Records
(Title - Road from Worst to Best)

Share your reviews on his

INSTAGRAM

@spicy_emotions
@shubham4shah

Or via email on

shubham2shah@gmail.com

To stay tuned to his work and opportunities follow his business Handles

INSTAGRAM FACEBOOK YOUTUBE

@flairsandglairs
@teekhezasbaaat

WEBSITE:

https://flairsandglairs.in/
https://flairsandglairs.com/

Ishani Agarwal

(Co-Founder- Flairs and Glairs)

Ishani Agarwal hails from the City of Joy, Kolkata.
She is the co -founder of her Community "Teekhe Zasbaaat" and Flairs and Glairs Publication.
Been a Compiler for 45+ Anthologies, she is in the process for more. Co-authored in 150+ Anthologies. She is a India Book of Records Holder, a Vajra World Records Holder, a High Range of Records Holder, an OMG Book of Records Holder, a Bravo Record holder, a Forever Star Book of World Records and an Indian Book of Records Holder.
Approved by Ne8x for its Lit Fest 2020, and Literary Icon 2020. Also a Golden Star Awards Winner 2020.
She has also been award ed with India Star Republic Award 2021, a part of She Awards by Awards Arc and Winner of Nari Samman 2021 by Literoma.

She is also selected as Best Achiever of the Year by AwardsArc and Most Challenging Compiler Award by Spectrum Awards.
She got her first solo Published,a solo Compilation consisting of first 750 contents of hers, titled "Hand That Burnt While Healing".

She has been featured by the National Magazine "Taree Zameen Par" with the title 'unstoppable'.
Also featured in the International Magazine DeMode for her upcoming solo novel, she is proud to write on social issues, and is happy with the love she is receiving.
Connect with her on Instagram: @Ishani_agarwal_quotes / @compilations_so_far

Shivangi Jaiswal
(Compiler)

Shivangi Jaiswal is a Content Writer from Kolkata. Executive Head at “Flairs & Glairs” brand with dynamics in events organizing and cultural educational pan INDIA. Organizer at "The Glittering Fables" Writing Community. She is a B. Com Honors graduate. Certified in Stocks & Short Selling as well as Certified in Digital Marketing student.
She is an Indian Book of Record Holder.

Approved by Ne8x for its Lit Fest 2020 for the Author of the Year 2020 and the Real Hero's Title 2020. Also, a Warrior of Change Awardee 2021.
Recently been awarded Writer of the year Award 2021 by Forever Star World book of Records.
She loves to bring smiles and happiness to many faces, so she is into social service.
Traveler, Teacher, Meditator, Dancer, Singer, Instrument Player. She loves to play guitar and harmonium. Also been awarded in many events for winning many categories Been a Public Speaker she has taken part in many events and nailed it. Been a great Advisor to many. She has also been crowned for winning Miss Grea t Podium 2020 Title in the category Modelling recently. Sports freak of Swimming and Badminton with a passion so strong. Since, past one year she has started her writing journey.
She writes so that many people can connect with their stories and get positi ve hopes. She thinks " Every story is unique so embrace yourself to the best". She is a writer by day and a reader by night. Been a Complier of 40+ Anthologies, and in process for more, also Co - authored 1 50+ anthologies. Shivangi is an old soul with young eyes, a vintage heart, and a beautiful mind."

You can follow her work:
Instagram
@the_knockingvibe
@house_of_compilations

5 Elements of Nature

God has made wonderful creations.
Nature's Five Elements thrive for life.

The smoothness of the air,
can disappear the sorrows away.

The purity of the water,
can destroy all our armor.

The elegant beauty of the sky,
no one can buy.

The purity and sparklines of the fire,
no one can acquire.

The suffering of the mother earth,
no one can ever pay off.

Everything is beautiful that flourishes, nourishes and
cherishes each and every beauty of nature.

Beauty of Nature

In the serene of beauty.
Craving of simplicity.
God gave us 5 beautiful elements of nature.

We ride on it,
search for truth in the divine fire.
Live in the happiness of joy that nature gives us.

Motivate and thank each day for such a heavenly life, along with the godly creation we always rise and shine.

With the beauty so pure and paths that overshine.
The life with wings for a rise of heaven to fly.

Dushyant Walia

This is Dushyant Walia
from Gurgaon, Haryana.
A social worker and a Civil Engineer by profession, working as blood coordinator in his group "Blood Donors Team NCR" since 2013 to help people in blood emergencies. It's a family of volunteers who always ready to serve humanity by their priceless efforts and unity. They pledge to serve their best in all possible way with their fellow coordinators of other cities in India to minimize deaths due to lack of blood.
Dushyant Walia (Er.)
Founder & Coordinator
Blood Donors Team NCR

दुनिया पंचतत्व की
(भूमि, जल, वायु, अग्नि व आकाश)

पांच तत्वों से मिलकर बनी है यह हसीन दुनिया,
जहां हर एक तत्व का अपना एक अहम हिस्सा है,

जिसमे सबसे पहले आती है हमारी पावन भूमि,
जिसका दुनिया मे बड़ा ही अनमोल किस्सा है,

दूसरे स्थान पर आता है ये पावन अनमोल जल,
जिसके बिना नही है हमारा आज और ना ही कल,

तीसरे स्थान पर आती है अब ये ताप अग्नि की,
जो कभी कभी तो बन जाती है कारण विनाश की,

चौथे स्थान पर आती है ये लहराती हुई वायु,
जीवन के लिए आवश्यक है देती है धिर्ग आयु,

अंतिम और पांचवे स्थान पर आता है आकाश,
जिसके जरिये होता है इस सारे जग में प्रकाश,

इन सबके बिना नही है शृष्टि का कोई स्वरूप,
पंचतत्व से बड़ा नही है दुनिया मे कोई भी रूप..!!

Shivansh Sharma

He is Shivansh Sharma. Basically, from Indore but perusing MBA (Marketing &Hr) in Mysore Karnataka. He always has a passion for writing the thoughts which come into his mind. A hardcore foodie as he belongs to Indore. He is the one who is always ready to help his near ones. His life revolves around his family and friends. He is always self -motivated, enthusiastic and a person with positive vibes. He is a ceauthor of 50+ books and a compiler of 2 book. currently holding the position of Ink Over Tears Group Admin in Flairs and Glairs. His only belief is just to live happily and enjoy every moment of life.

You can contact him on ig@shivanshrockzzzzz

वो आग

आहुति अपने आत्मविश्वास की
मन की उत्सुक आकांक्षाओं की
दे कर उसने क्या पाया ,एक सहज जीवन ।

सीधी रेखा सा नीरस
जल शांत ठहरा ना उथल पुथल ,
जिम्मेदारी दुनियादारी , ये ही उसकी होशियारी ।

ठंडी आग बची बस राख ,
भभूत समझ लगाए ,
ढोंगी रचाए , ज्ञानी होने का ।

उसी में लोट लगाए
बावरा जोगी , खुद ही हारे अपने मन को
जो कहीं बची हो थोड़ी सी आग
तो फिर आज हवा दे साहस की
फिर भड़का दे ले चले मशाल ।

पानी

पानी तेरी भी अलग पहचान है
जहा मिल जाए वो ही तेरा रंग , शान है
तेरी पहचान तेरी खामोशी है ,
तू बिन बोले बहुत कुछ कह देता है,
जैसे आज तक कभी वक्त ना रुका ,
वैसे ही तू भी कभी ना रुकता है ,
बस अपनी राह खुद बनाकर
चलते रहता है , बहता रहता है ,
है तू हर जगह समुद्र में शांत,
कुएं में रुककर सबकी प्यास बुझाता ,
तू ही सबका साथी तेरे होते सब आबाद है ,
तू रूद्र रूप में आकर सैलाब बन जाता
और खुश होता तो बारिश बन बरसता,
हर शक्स को बस तेरा ही आसरा है ,
ए पानी तू अमृत के समान ।

Raj Jot

Raj jot is an ambitious poet and a content writer with a creative mind. He is a lyricist also. He thinks writing is the best way to express yourself. He belongs to Chandigarh. He is currently working as a chef. A multi-talented person. He is passionate about exploring the world. He loves to interact with new people and wants to fulfil his all dreams.
You can follow him on Instagram @rajjotofficial

गंगा का पानी

यह पग पग पल पल बहती बनारस में गंगा
किनारों से टकराती चलती जाती है यह गंगा
खुशबू है इस गंगा के पानी में
यह कल-कल बहता पानी
यह मध्यम मध्यम से चलती हवा
वह जगमग जगमग करती रातें
थोड़ा सा झिलमिल झिलमिल करता शोर
यह है गंगा मेरे दोस्त
यह है गंगा मेरे दोस्त .
हिमालय की चोटी से चलती आती बहती आती गंगा
कभी टकराती तो कभी किसी से मिल जाती
कभी दिल को छू जाती
तो कभी प्यास को बुझा जाती है
अंत में जा कर यह समुंदर से मिल जाती
यह है गंगा मेरे दोस्त
यह है गंगा मेरे दोस्त

कुदरत

मेरी उम्र छोटी सी
उड़ान एक परिंदे की तरह
बादलों में घर बना के
समय से कुछ लफ्ज़ को उधार लेकर
आज मैंने कुदरत को लिखा ।

सपने थोड़े से बड़े लेकर
खयालो का एक मयान भरकर
मैंने कुदरत को थोड़ी करीब से देखा
देखा मैंने खिलते हुए फूलों को
और देखा मैंने आसमान में उड़ते हुए आजाद पंछियों को
उनकी खुशियों को लेकर थोड़ा सा उधार ,
आज मैंने कुदरत को अपनी डायरी के पन्नों पर लिखा ।

गंगा के पानी से लेकर समुंदर की उठती लहरों को
बारिश की बूंदों को मैंने चेहरे पर गिरते महसूस किया
सुबह की कोयल की कू कू से लेकर रात के सन्नाटे तक
सूरज की किरणों से लेकर चांद की चांदनी तक
मैंने कुदरत को है देखा ।
इस दिन से कुछ पल को उधार लेकर
मैंने अपनी डायरी के पन्नों पर कुदरत को लिखा

Vaishnavi Hend

Vaishnavi Hend hails in the orange city Nagpur (Maharashtra). She is a creator by habit, a microbiologist by occupation and an amateur writer by her own choice. She has done lots of anthologies along with a world record anthology. She is also compiling her own anthologi es named "Blink To Think" And "This Is My Story". You can get to her by typing Blink2Think-B2T on YouTube and blink2think_insta_official on Instagram.

Fire of Passion

Fire is said to be a destructive adamant cosmic element
Fire is also expressed as an intense feeling of vehement
But fire has the constructive ability too
You will only resonate with this, if you really have that fire of passion within you
You are passionate about this, you are passionate about that
But did you ever experience your real fir e of passion to which you are actually passionate at?
So, for the correct answer, you first need to know what the fire of passion is
It's the sparkling fiery energy that keeps us going
It's our excitement and happiness which while doing that specific work we are showing
It's the powerful bomb of anticipation in fulfilling anything you set your mind to
It is the real meaning of life that keeps us filled with meaning in everything we do
Take it as a clarification not as a classification
Because to be passionate about something is the real fire of passion

To have that sparkling fire is a good addiction
It's the state of intense desire without any condition
Feel the power in you,
See what comes from focusing on what excites you
With a little concentration
Understand the thing that passion is the real passion
With no competition, zero aggression,
Full of impassion and a little-little compassion
Focus on all these things and make confession to yourself
About your real fire of passion without any confusion
Because to be passionate about something is the real fire of passion

Sahina Ghugha

Sahina Ghugha is 20-year-old b.com student at Saurashtra university Rajkot. She is from Jamnagar city of Gujarat. She is state level winner in poetry competition 2017. She is Co - author of 15+ anthologies. She is an amazing writer and poet and she wants do something for society through her pen.
Insta ID: - Itz_Sahina_write

पंचतत्व के पांच पर्यायी

पृथ्वी हर जीवन को कुछ देती है।
धरती मां सबके दुःख हर लेती है।
भूमि पे बढ़ते प्रदूषण से हो रही ये बेजान है।
ज़मीन के बिना कहां उगता धान है?
वसुंधरा तेरा हम पे बड़ा एहसान है।

पानी बिना कोई जीवन नहीं है।
जल है ये कोई उपवन नहीं है।
नीर की बूंदों से सागर का आहवान है।
सलिल बिना शरीर में कहां जान है?
वारि तेरा हम पे बड़ा एहसान है।

आग में ऐसी अनोखी प्रचंड ताकत है।
पावक है ये जलकर भी देता राहत है।
अनल के पास तप का अखंड ज्ञान है।
अग्नि की साक्षी में दिया जाता महादान है।
वहि तेरा हम पे बड़ा एहसान है।

वायु अपनी धून में ऐसे है बहेता।
पवन हर मिट्टी का दाग है सहेता।
समीर से सांसे ,रगो में जान है।
हवा से ही तो चलता ये जहान है।
अनिल तेरा हम पे बड़ा एहसान है।

आकाश के सितारे लगते है प्यारे।
अंबर में जुमते सूरज, चंदा न्यारे।
गगन के पास सारी चीज़े महान है।
नभ ही तो हमारा अविरत आसमान है।
फलक तेरा हम पे बड़ा एहसान है।

राशिका

लेखक रशीका कक्षा 12वी की छात्रा है उसे शायरी एवं कविता लिखने का शौक है इसके अलावा उसे चित्रकारी करना भी पसंद है
लेखिका के अनुसार:
अकेला होना ही अच्छा है, कम से कम कोई होगा नहीं तुम्हें दर्द देने।

(1)

ये धरती हमसे कितना कुछ बतलाती है
आपने हर जज़्बात को ये दर्शाती हैं
अपनी खुशी को खिलते नवजीवन से जताती है
मायूस हो तो बरखा बन बरस जाती है
अलास में आकर शीतल पुरवाई बहाती है
तो गुस्सा होकर समुंदर में तांडव मचाती है
और हर दम अपनी ममता का एहसास कराती हैं।

(2)

भ्रमांड के हर तत्व की अपनी अलग विशेषता है
पानी शीतल है तो पवन जरा प्रबल
अग्नि जरा गर्म तो आसमान जरा नम्र
भूमि की तो बात निराली है
कब सूखा तो कभी छाई हरियाली है
अलग है पर भी जुड़े रहते है
अनेकता में एकता का प्रमाण देते हैं।

Sneha Ahuja

Sneha is an avid explorer, who loves to look beyond the sky. Currently pursuing her interest in science, along with her love for penning thoughts into composes. She believes that life is the opportunity of being better than yourself.

She

She gave me so much,
I know I can't ever repay.
She feels like home,
She is the ground where I stay.

She goes so deep.
My feet can't touch,
This ocean bed.
She is the water over my head,
I will drown but won't dread.

She gave me all the space,
I'll ever need,
To balance all my energy.
We make amazing synergy.
And now I look up on the sky,
And I feel like she is seeing me.
She blows the wind through my hair,
Moves across her white cloudy wear.

She is the golden blazing fire,
She is the feeling of love and warmth.
But when she's gone, I feel the chills,
I feel alone while looking through the hills.

So, if you find her, tell her,
"I've been looking everywhere."
I lost the nature and all of its five elements.
She is the earth, she is the water,
Space, wind and fire.
She is the only one, I'll ever desire.

Aishwarya Umashankar

An enthusiastic person with a positive spirit towards everything. Hailing from Tamilnadu with a vision to experience, enjoy and succeed in every task taken. Lives with a moto 'Short life with a big world to enjoy. Hence Never accept anything low'. Rising with love for world and nature and blooming in the form of poetries at her Instagram handle __uv_says.

Here's the one from the bottom of her heart to emphasis the beauty of all the elements we are surrounded by and how man transformed them! Enjoy the journey through this poem!

Elements and The Life

All through the eras the world was silent
With every element just away from the other.
Getting them closer made the environment violent
and destroyed one another.
As fire met water
And the earth met space,
there were just steam and remnants shattered!
Thus, everything remained at peace only at a distance!
With a zeal to feel, water made fish
that jumped to speak with the land
And the land gave birth to a life with a wish
to drench its deserted sand.
The clever life molded stones and handled fire
to set it to reach the space pacing through air!
The admired space to see the life with desire
melted down as water through air!
The water drenched the land
and quenched its thirst.
It poured upon fire that revert back as steam
to touch the space with love.
Ultimately all elements loved and merrily mingled together
with the life
Which was then named "Man “!

Kalamkaar

This is Kalamkaar. He is from Uttrakhand bought up in Meerut (Up). His hobbies are reading and writing. His interest is in writing. He loves writing. He is part of 390+ Anthologies as Co-Author. He won 400+ Certificate in Writing, He Start writing 29 February 2020. He is part of 5 anthology as Co Author going for record and He is omg record holder as Co - Author of Book Called Laposia. He is simple and people observer. His insta handle is kalamkaar51 and email is kalamkaar51@gmail.com. He believes in Karma.

पंच तत्व में मिल जायेगा

घमंड किस बात का करता हैं, कुछ नहीं साथ लेके जाएगा!
रहेगा सब यही पे, बुरा वक़्त आया तो लुफ्त भी नहीं उठा पायेगा!
अपने ऐशो आराम को कहाँ तू साथ लेके जायेगा!
सब यही धारा का धारा रह जायेगा और तू एक दिन पंच तत्व में मिल जायेगा!
सबसे मिलते रहो बात करते रहो दिल में मैल रखने से कुछ नहीं पायेगा!
बुरे वात में साथ होगा नहीं कोई अकेला तू भटकता रह जायेगा!
मिला नहीं क्यों नहीं किसी से में इस बात का अफ़सोस मनाएगा!
अंत समय में कुछ नहीं कर पायेगा और पंच तत्व में मिल जायेगा!
सबका भला करो किसी का बुरा करने से तू क्या पायेगा!
कर्म का फल मिलेगा ऊपरवाले से नहीं बच पायेगा!
बुराई ही बुराई सबसे हर वक़्त पायेगा!
रिश्ता नहीं रहेगा तेरे से अकेला तू रह जायेगा, मिलने कोई नहीं तुझसे आएगा अगर तू पंच तत्व में भी मिल जायेगा!
गिरा अगर किसी की नज़रो से तो कहाँ उठ पायेगा!
दिल से निकला अगर किसी के तो कहाँ जगह दोबारा पायेगा!
बेरुखी रहेगी मन में सबको तेरे लिए तेरा कोई भला नहीं चाहेगा!
और ये गम तू संभाल नहीं पायेगा और पंच तत्व में मिल जायेगा!
कोई नहीं रहता धरती में उसकी मर्ज़ी के बिना कुछ नहीं हो पायेगा!
अच्छे कर्म होंगे तेरे तू रहमत तेरे पे वो बरसायेगा!
याद रहेगा सबके दिल में तेरे जाने के बाद अफसोस भी जताया जायेगा!
जाना सबको हैं मगर ज़िंदा यादो में जायेगा,भले ही दिन पंच तत्व में तू मिल जाएगा!

Shruti Dash

A techie by profession, and poet of the collection "The Memory Entourage: intoxicated by memories". A little quirky, mostly sincere, an overthinker –some might say; she has a habit of noticing the slightest optimism, even in pensive situations. Why does she write? She has the gift of poise and motivation to share.

Her creations on Instagram are just a search away. Find @the_element_of_immortality.

The below poem is dedicated to a special person in her life who chose the love of nature over worldly existence.

The Ocean's Gift

A gust of wind blew in front of him.
He was as amazed by it as he was
by the sand beneath him.
Droplets of ocean water touching him
and then a tide came rushing at him.
He was afraid at first but later
embraced the saltiness of the water.

That's the beauty of nature, isn't it?
As a person who had not gotten out
of her home since 4 years, he was
renewed by this experience.
The golden beach brought gold into
his life which co-existed with nature.
He felt nurtured.
He felt loved.

Now he is capable of loving herself.
How does he do it you ask?
He closes his eyes and imagines his world.
He imagines the cosmic elements of nature
that brought him back to happiness.

He imagines the cold touch of ocean water
at night when he was with himself and God.
He was with the very person who created all this.
He is still with Him.
He chose to stay with Him instead of me.
He chose to stay away from all of us.

I do not know what compelled him
to rush to the clouds.

Maybe, he wanted to experience
the source of rain.
He wished to be with the purest
form of nature.
The purest air, the cleanest water.
He already had the fire within him.
He has definitely left his mark on Earth.
Now, he also achieved the thunderous
courage to be what he wished.

He is now one with Lazarus.

Shradha Gindlani

Hailing from a small town with big dreams, Shradha Gindlani is a teacher in profession and a writer in her inner callings. She has compiled anthology ' Bitter Truth ' and 'Back to Nursery' and has been a co -author in a number of anthologies. With a vision of a community aiming at serving ones in need and upholding those who are part of it, she makes it to be humble and kind hearted. You can reach her Instagram handle at @creatorcreates18

For He Is There

While my deeds were dusty
His grace was pure air
To my fierce and fired 'myness'
His humility pours water
As
To serve the union in the space
For he is there

Rushda

Born on 19th October 2001 to Mrs. Shabnoor (a teacher) and Mr. Anwar Ahmad (a Business Man) Rushda is a native of Gonda, Uttar Pradesh. Aft er successfully completing her schooling she moved to New Delhi, Delhi and is currently pursuing her graduation in Mathematics.

Rushda is optimistic and spreads her charm wherever she goes. She loves painting, crafting, gardening and travelling. Writing is one of her hobby. Despite not being completely devoted to writing, she is praised for her poetic sense by many.

She has written many write ups and has been a part of various anthologies.

For feedbacks and suggestions feel free to contact her at the mail ID ansarirushda.ra@gmail.com

The Human Body

Who are we?
What is our existence?
Are we just mere body?
What are we here for?
My mind questions.
Running behind achieving our material goals,
We never know where it will lead us.
Day in day out we keep losing our identity.

Let us understand ourselves.

We are the Earth.
Born to spread goodness.
To bring positivity.
To do love and respect all.
To realize our true potentials.

We are Water.
Born to purify this world.
To be gold and amplifier.
To be present without boasting.
To save the entire humanity.

We are Fire.
Born to burn bad omens.
To stand against all wrongs.
To destroy what is destructing.
To keep rising above all odds.

We are Air.
Born to rejuvenate broken souls.
To touch our inner souls.

To leave a soothing effect.
To learn to clean what's dirty.

We are the Space.
Born to be infinite.
To absorb all energies.
To radiate love and charm.
To accept all that comes.

Let us now love ourselves.

Identify your true self.
Pursue your ultimate goals.
Let us not simply fade away.
Play your assigned roles perfectly.
Show your inner beauty.
Let go all your bad vibes.
Simply radiate positivity.
Just love, love and love.

Ravi Ahirwar

I'm Ravi Form Guna, MP.
Educated in Bsc

मैं, मैं हूं। तुम, तुम हो।

मैं चलती हवा का एक,
छोटा सा झोंका हूं
तुम तूफान से आने वाली
एक बड़ी सी आंधी हो

मैं बारिश की एक
छोटी सी बूंद की तरह हूं
तुम भी उसी बारिश की
बड़ी सी बाढ़ की तरह हो

(हवा-पानी सबको चाहिए
काम एक ही है बस स्वरूप
अलग अलग है)

क्योंकि शायद मैं, मैं हूं।
तुम, तुम हो।

Vikash Kumar Bhakat

About the poet

Vikash Kumar Bhakat is writer, author novelist, and social & educational entrepreneur from Shankarda village near Jamshedpur, Jharkhand.

The poet is also the President of Vikash Educational & Charitable Trust. The author runs an English school where free English education is imparted to the poor underprivileged students at Janamdih a tribal dominated village under potka block of East Singhbhum district of Jharkhand.

The Earth

All the creatures live in the earth
Whether big or small all live in the earth
Everyone has to die in the earth
We need air and water to live in the earth
Round is the earth
All the creatures take birth in the earth
We get results according to our deeds in the earth
The almighty God protects the earth
We need to plant trees to save the earth
It has tranquility and prosperity
If we live in it with unity
The has beautiful mountains, hills, oceans and rivers.

Air, Water and Fire

Two different things in nature
Air is invisible indeed
We can sense its presence
Fire and air play significant role in the earth
Both are violent and mannerly as well
They are quite sincere do their duties so well
Fire and air are equally important to us
They have their own recognition
No one can deny their devotion
Air and water needed to extinguish fire
Water quenches our thirst
Air and water are required for survival of any living beings
Air, Water and Fire so useful things in the earth

Riya Srivastava

Poet by passion and entrepreneur by action. My word and my creation is to express my feelings to others and connect with the emotions of the people. Follow me on Instagram@riyashrivastava2000.

पंचतत्व

तत्व हैं ये पाँच, पर है बहुत ही खास
जिनसे निर्माण हुआ इस संसार का
जो साक्षी है हर नए काम का।
उत्पत्ति इसी से, मिलना इसी में
कोई छेड़छाड़ जो किया इनसे
मिल जाता है खाक में।
जल ,वायु, मिटटी, आकाश, धरती है नाम इनके
एक सृष्टि के निर्माण का आधार है
इन्ही से जीवन इन्ही से मरण
इन्ही से सारा संसार है।

Ashwini Singh

He is Ashwini, a budding pharmacist from Delhi. He has been writing quotes and poems since long back but never thought of writing them for publication purpose. It is due to his friend that he has entered in this field. He is very thankful to that friend of his.

अग्नि

मैं धरित्रि के अंतर का ज्वार ,
मैं प्रलय का अमिट नाद ,
शंकर की त्रिनेत्र मे शुशोभित , दीप्त विद्यमान हूं ,
तिमिर मे अंतर - प्रकाश के तेज पुंज समान हूं ,
मैं प्रकृति के तत्वों में प्रधान अग्नि हूं ।।

दिवाकर सा प्रखर तेजवान हूं ,
सागर सा उन्मत्त प्रलय वान हूं ,
वीरों के पराक्रम सा जवाजल्यामान हूं ,
दुर्गा के उन्मत्त हास के समान हूं ,
हां मै प्रकृति के तत्वों में प्रधान अग्नि हूं ।।

Muskan Sachdeva

Muskan sachdeva hails from basti, uttar pradesh. she completed studies from st. basil's and is pursuing chartered accountant along with BCom from allahabad university. writing was just a time pass earlier but then it became her passion. she has been co-authored in 50+ anthologies.

The Five Elements

The five cosmic elements namely Earth, Water, Fire, Air and Space commonly known in India as Pirthvi, Pani, Aag, Vayu and Antariksh. Each have a different meaning and a different purpose. They are used in spells, rituals and prayers. Although in different cultures, each have a different meaning, purpose and even more elements. Each element can represent different ritual tools, herbs, candles, crystals, natural objects, zodiac signs, etc.

These links provide us with some details: -

Earth's season is winter and its direction is north.

Air's season is spring and its direction is east.

Fire's season is summer and its direction is south.

Water's season is autumn and its direction is west.

Spirit is everywhere and it connects all the elements.

Abhilash Sharma

Abhilash Sharma a 24-year-old passionate writer. He belongs to Sonipat, Haryana. He had completed his B.com (voc) recently. He is an enthusiastic person and a sports lover as well. Worked as a coauthor in about 50+ anthologies inspired by Ishika Arora and Ishani Aggarwal in the field of writing. You can check out his writings on Instagram at @_ankahe_alfaaz__ .

पंच तत्व:- ज़िन्दगी का हिस्सा

ज़िन्दगी का एक अनोखा सा हाथ ,
जिसका रहता हैं हमेशा साथ ,
चाहे दिन हो या हो रात ,
बिना उसके होती ना कोई बात ,

हम सबको संभाला तो धरती माता कहलाई ,
आगे बढ़ने की राह अग्नि ने बनाई ,
विचारों की भाषा पानी ने सिखाई ,
मंज़िलों की मशाल वायु ने जलाई

जब ज़िन्दगी की उपलब्धियां आसमान में छाई ,
ऐसे ही हमने दुनिया में इज़्ज़त है कमाई ।।

Anwesa Chakraborty

She is Anwesa Chakraborty, pursuing VFX (Visual Effects) from Hi-Tech Animation, Shyambazar, lives in Kolkata, West Bengal, India. Completed her Graduation, from University of Calcutta in 2019, after that she started writing. Also, a photographer, but not professional, because she loves to capture what she likes and finds interesting, nature soo thes her, and greenery gives her peace. Thus, most of her writings and poems are based on nature, uses very simple language that everyone can understand. She has been a part of some Anthologies named L'amour – compiled by Nikhil Jain, Nisha Tiwari and Jayashree Sunkari in 2020 and Confession Beyond Curtain & Khubsurat Safar in 2021. Her writing has a touch of abstract feature, which is appreciated by all. You can find her writings and connect with her on Instagram - @the_parrot_says, E-mail - chakrabortyanwesa@gmail.com

Nature's Energy

The world is full of happiness, cheerfulness and more of natural vibes. This world is created by the beauty of mother nature, which we preserve with ourself in the form of 'drawing' 'sketching', 'photography', 'music' and 'writing'. All these activities come by visualization, if one can visualize things in detail then only the output would be realistic. Now, these words are not only a word, these are energies, produced by mother nature.

Cosmic Elements are : AIR, WATER, EARTH, SPACE, FIRE. All these five elements are directly related to our daily life in again some different form or are packed in a beautiful word, like our bones are packed by the skin. , these elements produces energy and are converted to the above mentioned forms.

These elements also impact our cultural tradition. Indians eat by hands by digging fingers on the food and then to our palette, and by this all these five elements are passed to our body. Our five fingers depict these five elements i.e. index finger – AIR, middle finger – SPACE, ring finger – EARTH, little finger – WATER, thumb finger – FIRE. Thus, if we visualize in a different perspective as per our tradition, we are more energetic.

Let us now discuss about the significance of the elements in a creative way. Space, it signifies the volume and vastness, which is converted into our vast thinking capacity. Earth, it signifies preservation which is converted to be creative with what we have. Air, it signifies purity which is converted to our duration of life. Water and Fire, these are interconnected, without water we can't live and without fire we would not feel

warmth. Water is like the supporting element to cool down ourselves when our anger re aches its utmost level. And we bounded by all these elements, or can be said a total universe in one body.

Sonal Saha

Since childhood she learned from her experience related to life, failure and wisdom more than she learned from her academic's life.
She used to write her pain, her happiness in her diary due to which she found more deeper connection in writing, reading poets and novels. This small things for her becomes the most precious thing to her.
She is also engaged in professional course i.e Co mpany Secretary.

"The Elements"

The creation of the creature is beyond the imagination for all of us. From the beginning of the universe to the unsolved mystery of the space there were some elements which will be presented from the starting to the ending and will also going to be remained even if the destruction has taken place all over.

To understand the creation of the creature, it itself required a great level of understanding, a devotion towards our mother - nature, a love towards our nature. As we all are not the apart from the universe, instead, we all are the part of the universe. The universe is inside of all of us in the form of the elements i.e Earth, Water, Fire, Air and Space.

As we take vegetables, fruits from the trees and plants they were grounded by the "Earth" Only.
As we take water to drink, but our own body are made up of 75% of "Water".
As the "Fire" Itself known for its purity, we all are also possessed the purity in the form of honesty.
As the "Air" Itself has the magic we can't see it but then too we can't be alive without it. We all are connected with the air also in the form of our breathe.
As the "Space" Itself indicates the freedom, we can't hold it. Similarly, we all are also seeking space in our relationships too.

We all are not different from our cosmic elements but instead we all are the cosmic elements...!!

Ami Patel

She is Ami Patel from Ankleshwar 25 years old. She is writer, poet and book reviewer. She loves travelling. Her writing comes out of her feelings of her deepest relationships and its purity. She is also available on youtube to share her views and writing. She works in human resource dep artment. She appreciates life with its all perspectives. You can give her review about her writing on Instagram @amipatel95

तत्व से

सब रंगो को अपनाने वाले पानी से बन जाओ
या अंतर में धधकती ज्वाला से सख्त बन जाओ
ठंडी नरम हवा से कभी मेरे साथ बह चलो
या सरल आकाश की तरह सब जगह मुझसे आ मिलो
मैं बन जाऊँ वो पृथ्वी जिसके पास तुम सँभलने आ जाओ

Dipti David

Dipti is a budding author who aspires to publish a book under her name. She is an avid reader. She loves listening to music and doodling. She has contributed to several anthologies. And she has her own book blog and general blog. She is preparing for NET a nd exploring all types of writing. She is currently residing in Madurai.

Heading to the Cosmos

Latha was a girl who was passionate about astronomy. She loved to gaze at the stars which appear in the night sky. She was curious about the shifting shapes of the moon.
And she was mesmerized by its beauty each night. She wondered how the surface of the moon a nd stars would feel like.

She wanted to go into outer space. And travel to other planets and galaxies. She dearly wished for that to happen some day when a shooting star crossed at that moment. After admiring the beautiful night sky for a longtime, she went and lied down to sleep for the night.

She went into deep sleep and had a vision, where she woke up to see something that really amazed her. She was in a spacesuit and was also inside spaceship. She was travelling into the outer space where she could see a billion stars with Jupiter, Venus, and Mars around with a thick black background.

At first, she couldn't figure out what was happening. But after few seconds she realized that she was in space. Seeing this she got overly excited. And was about to jump with joy but suddenly she started flying. And that was a moment she was enjoying like anything. She flew all around the spaceship while shouting as a result of being overcome with Joy. And when the spaceship landed on the moon, she came out of the spaceship and started jumping on the surface of the moon.

(2)

She was enjoying her small visit to the moon where everything is white and powdery. She wanted to touch the soft glowing surface of the amazingly white moon.So, as she was bouncing here and there, she got into the spaceship to go to the planet Jupiter. And as Latha got into the spaceship she was about to start it. But suddenly she woke up to see a ray of sunlight glistening its glorious morning light straight on her face.

At that moment she realized that it was just a dream. She was happy that she had the dream but sad that it was not real. So, she got up and started going about her day's business. But she was very much interested in space science and aeronautical engineering. She read a lot on that subject. And she wanted to become an Astronaut.

And later on, when she came to college and persuade Aeronautical engineering and space related studies. After completing her studies. She applied for a job at NAZA. And she got the job. Although it was a small job and she struggled in it for a very long time. She never let go of it and worked hard. Since she was passionate about going intospace, she did a lot of smart work.

She gradually reached the top position and kept working on her goal towards her dream job.
One day out of the blue cameher job opportunity of going into space as an Astronaut. She was one among the seven members who went into space. While she was in the spaceship, she enjoyed marveling at the splendid wonder of the cosmos. Her first venture was successful.

As days went by, Latha also progressed in her career. She has done a lot of research about the particles in the cosmos and has ventured into many galaxies. And she has visited many planets.

Kehinde Margret Makinde

Makinde Kehinde Margret is poet, has several works on Poetizer by the pen name “Abadan Omooba” and written for people on contract basis.
She lives in Ile -Ife, Osun State, Nigeria and does “Spiritual mentoring and counseling”. She has won the Siwes Essay Competition (Serra Club of Ibadan, Nigeria 2015.
She Has a degree in Law from the Obafemi Awolowo University, Ile-Ife, Osun State, Nigeria.

Nature

The heart of existence, who can know
In the eyes of empathy, society and affection
In the ears of interaction and context
On the earth space and humanoid pavement.
Water! Oh! how precious
Natural, relinquishing, greater good exploration
The stimulator in complex-success
Estimate of flowing free will on tongues.
The burnout, the fatigue of you
Keep us warm,
more blessings than blasting cruelty
perpetually embracing the chefs 'goals
Keep candles burning.
Air! Oh, how affectionate
The enhancer of feelings, vulnerability and power
Yet element most ignored
How mutual, loyal, lovely and resilient
In Softness and skill, best of hope and existence.

Payal Indani

Co- author Payal Indani is a heartborn girl with lots of love in her eyes. Heartbroken by her loved one. Still finds love in everyone. She is happy with whatever she has and also desires to be an author of her own book very soon. Love legal practices but firmly interested in reality of everything. She wants to achieve the nano happiness in life and be a star of her own family like a gem. She is Co-author in almost a dozen of anthologies and seeks the opportunities in every way she could.

Sparkle

Cosmic elements are the sparkles of the life. Earth, where we reside, is the only source of us being alive. It's well said, "Mother Earth", because, despite of all, earth is our first mother. Water and fire become the body parts of our mother earth. All such cosmic elements are being required by us t o survive on this planet. The important one could be - water. Particularly, waste is considered to be the basic necessity and it is true.

(2)

Space is likely to be defined for many of the combinations. Whether it might be actual space, or emotional spa ce or whatever it may be. As the eternal feeling of love is required to live a life, likewise all the cosmic elements are the most important part of our survival. As a fire can light up things, it can also destroy it if things go out of control. This actually is about life. If things go out of control, everything will be destructed soon. All we need to do is, preserve and love.

M.Haseebunissa

M. Haseebunissa is a young, aspiring and a vibrant leader holding sound knowledge in theoretical and practical aspects of counselling. She holds a Masters in Applied Psychology and is currently pursuing her Master of Philosophy in Counselling. She is a certified NLP Prac titioner and a Licensed Emotional Intelligence Coach Practitioner. She loves to write and believes in the magic of words to transform lives. She finds solace in writing. Her work at various domains involves promoting optimal mental health.

The Undying Fire

And it's the fire in you
That lead you to places
You have never been;
Takes you to journeys
You have forever longed.

And it's the fire within you
That makes you glow
A little more;
Sparkles your eyes
And creates a vision.

And it's the same fire
That keeps burning in you
Which you build yourself with.
It's the same fire!

Gurdeep Kaur

Hobby - writing and playing games

Earth, Air, Water, Fire and Space =Human Body

A body is great tool
Gifted by God to us
N to our soul
Cause of this we
Can do everything
We want to do
Like
-A writers
With eyes we saw
The Beauty of
Everything around us
With mind we create
With hand we put
That creation on paper
-A singers
Writer lyrics and sing
And present it to their fans
-A chef they invent
New dishes daily
For everyone
-A farmer
They work every day
In any season for
Food for everyone
-A designer
They create new design
And make dresses
-A scientist
They always try to
Create something
New to help our country
Human mind is very important tool

Without mind we are dumb
With mind we can create daily
New items for people around us

Priya Srivastava

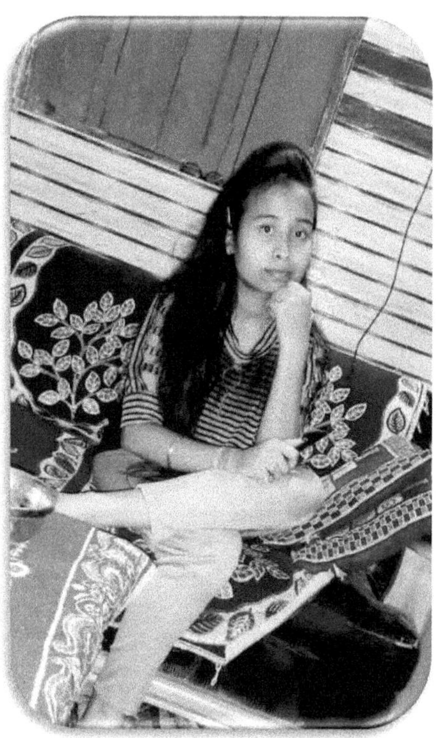

Hello dear, I'm Priya Srivastava. I grew up in Lucknow, and lived there most of my life before moving. I love write-up and study new things.

The Cosmic Elements-A, F,E,W,S

A mother Where are we come from to whom we return
You nurture us protect us in the......
Harsh of the conditions Feed us in the womb....
Oh! Mother nature No one can surpass your generosity.....
You nurture and keep us in your cradle while we humans...
Are sucking and corrupting you with all our monstrosity....
Like Earth, build upon A foundation of facts.....
Like Air, Be willing to change your ideas..
If winds of evidence require it Like Fire, be unquenched in......
A desire for learning more.Like Water, both our ideas.......
Fire wants to burn Water wants to flow....
Air wants to rise Earth wants to bind....
Chaos wants to devour Cal wants to live.....
Don't dismiss the elements Water soothes and heals....
Air refreshes and revives Earth grounds and holds.....
Fire is a burning reminder Our own will and creative power.....
Swallow their spells There's a certain sweet comfort....
Knowing that you belong to them all
Be like the ancient elements in thinking.....
We are touched by you You scald and burn us as a reminder....
To the raging presence Ready to devour our pity existence....
You can turn the existence A mighty forest to fistful of ashes...
Pop the bubbles of pain and anxiety Meet a new you every day
Water Oh! Holy water You come in so many forms.....
The spaces between us and spaces Within us the ten door our soul makes..
The exit from And becomes one with the divine
The spaces us
and spaces within us.Boundless as our dreams bright and spangled
With our hopes you surround us and encompass us...
.....

Sushmita Ray Choudhury

Hi it's Sushmita, she's 17 years and she express her every feeling of life through words and in form of poetry and she feels happy and bless doing that. She's writing poems since she was of 7 or 8 years, she had lost track to that after few years but then when she took another shot, she understood she can do it. And she also loves to write songs, sing and play guitar, read novels and much more. She's very happy that her poem is getting published because it's like dream come true. And she believes in a quote of writer it's "A real writer can satisfy everyone's thirst but not themselves, that's the real one". Thank you and she hope you enjoy her poem.

Cosmic Beauty

The cosmic play of universe
Walking upon the 5 elements
Air, water, earth, fire and space
Are same since several ages
I call it the "Cosmic Beauty"
For reasons we rely on it

The air we breathe is versatile
The water we drink is divine
The earth we live upon is huge
The fire we have in earth's core
Is so perfectly devotional
The space that holds all together
Is the most phenomenal

The perfect portion of all
Dwell and makes beautiful world
All the precious beads together
Bind up in a string
Makes this whole world
A beautiful jewelry by deeds
By which creator of the universe
Our holy God succeeds

The love it gets poured
In each being's body
Reflects the power of lord
He used in creating each soul
The natural phenomenon occurs
By all grace of the cosmic beauty

The crazy creatures of universe

Created each piece of this world
And the 5 essence of all beauty
Are the perfect blessings so
I call it the "Cosmic Beauty"

Neeti Yadav

Neeti Yadav is an ordinary person with an extraordinary connection with emotions. She is an engineering graduate with a passion of penning down.

(1)

The cosmic elements and analogy with life
The human life
seems complicated
yet is easy.
Like water,
one must flow
to be happy
no matter what.
Fire is something
to keep alive
the spirit of trying!
One must get shaped
In life like wood
to be of use.
Lustrous and versatile
as metal,
one must be everything.
Lastly, earth loves all
And so should we.
That's how the cosmic
Elements are one of us.

Shivani Priyanga

Shivani Priyanga a 21-year-old proud citizen of Tanjavur, has a knack for words and an amazing flair in the Tamil Language. Though her choice for higher studies had become Engineering, she had endeavored to sculpt her writing style. Her only goal in life is to make her parents proud and she would work hard, going to any extent for them to have a prideful smile. She is a voracious reader having her choices revolve around English and Tamil Literature, but she says that particularly Cenmozhi has captivated her heart and writing in it has been the only cathartic experience throughout her life.

Mail: shivanipriyanga@gmail.com
Instagram: shivani_priyanga_quotes
Your quote: Shivani Priyanga

Nature Writes

The pink and blue skies
Travelled along with roaming flies!
The boiled yellow sun changing to Fried 65,
The moon along with its friends felt shy!
Foreign birds migrate,
With the pen & a cup of tea I ate!
Sea started shouting,
When my pen bleeds ink!
On the shore of sand,
Kids built a home with hand!
The Breeze,
Got Freeze!
Again, the Sky started roaming,
With the clouds having black ink!
I love the way,
That the air enters the bay!
For the fun of love,
I wonder to bow!
The nature,
It's the Future!
Moon is calling me,
Sea is making to see!
For the 7 wonders,
The 5 wing thunders!
Birds started humming,
Portraits a home coming!
The sound of happiness,
Executes the level of craziness!
The world is filled with psycho,
And we are letting it go!
The mountain scenery,
The field Greenery!

The eternity,
The fertility!
Of lands,
Of Grands!
The Granary,
Which is our honory!
The moon light,
& the Trend Fight!
Thus,
She teaches the Black & White lessons of lives!

Komal Singh

Komal Singh was born on 19 June 2004. Coauthor is a good writer from New Delhi. She is completing her schooling in commerce stream. She is writing quotes or stories for 1 year as her passion. She wants to be Writer and Bank PO.

The Five Elements of Nature

In Sanskrit five elements of nature are known as 'PANCHTATVA.' It originates from Sanskrit word 'panch' that means five and tatva which means elements.
The entire universe is created by the five elements. Everything we can see, touch or feel in nature is made up of these five elements. The body structure is made up of the elements.
The five basic elements of nature are known as 'Panchamahabhutas' which inhere the property of earth(prithvi), water(jal), fire (aag or tejas), wind(vayu) and space(akasha). Our human bod y is also made by these elements. These elements can be linked to human beings as - body as earth, water as mind, fire as intelligence, air as awareness and space as consciousness.
Title (writeup 2)
As we all know that earth is the third planet from the sn, other than this Earth is our home planet. The Earth is rigid, heavy and stable. It represents solidness. It is the 5th largest planet in the solar system. Earth's population is about 7 billion. It includes 71% of water and 29% of land. Earth includes s oil, landscape, flora and fauna etc.

Water is the second most important element of nature which is transparent, tasteless and odorless. It represents coldness. It helps to lubricate cohesive property. It is essential for all. Earth is made up of 71% wate r. Without water no one can live on the Earth. Every person, animal and plant need water for their survival. Even water plays an important role in the world economy.

Fire is an important process that affects ecological system around the globe. It signifi es heat that makes things mature, assists in melting and purification. It has the power to burn

and transform. Heat, passion and anger are assisted by fire. It represents the energy that can be transformed into other types of energy. It is connected to the flow of energy.

Air refers to the earth's atmosphere. The Air signifies the unstable movement, cold and dry. Air is the mixture of many gases and tiny dust particles. It has the essential thing in which living beings or living things can breathe and su rvive. Other than this air is the mixture of so many gases like nitrogen, oxygen, carbon dioxide etc. from which we are able to live.

Space means akasha, it is everything that lies above the surface of the Earth. It defines the gap between the twothings and it is also the element of non-resistance. So many natural phenomena can be seen in the space which are lightning, clouds, rainbow etc.

Reshma Sultana

She is passionate about her work. She loves helping people. She wants her life to be like water. Which is very much essential in everybody's life. She is cool and silent. She Is a social worker. She has done many social activities with silence. She has helped many needy people in their daughter's marriage. What she wants to earn is only blessings that will be benefited for her child.

Water

Feel the beauty in a drop of water
Boast power with the flow of water

Timeless beauty hard to ignore
Water is life.... That is pure

The pebbles on the shore keep on moving
Grow with honour.....like water
In the moon light shining.

You are in cloud, you are in ocean
You are vein, you are in rain.

You are clean and cool
Living in river and moving in pool.

Without you, there is no life
You are precious,
Say a thirsty. You are delicious

Avneet Kaur

She is a girl who let her writing express all the intense emotion she feels.

Emotions As The Five Elements

Emotions, a thing never about enough
Some people easily express it, some find it tough
Emotions are never limited, nor insignificant
Bet, there are emotions, humans still haven't discovered a name for
But it exists and people feel do experience it and that's not a coincident
Emotions are like five elements of nature; they are present in us but nobody can be sure
Fire is mostly likeanger; it burns out people inside and outside
It makes us stubborn and can make their loved one suffer and dried
Air resembles of jealousy, it can make a person do their best,
If used with precaution in right direction
It can also kill people by mixing with poison, if lost the sense of direction
Water reminds me of crying, it can save people if they let their negative emotions out by it
But it can also make a person completely drained, if that's the only thing they gonna do and just sit
Earth seems more like solitude and rigid, solitude can help people know who they truly are
But sometimes, it alsocreates distance between them and their loved ones and make them a bit sour
Spaces is like our brain, it holds everything in it, everything moving at their own speed
Sometimes it is still and happy Sometimes its exploded with intense emotions and won't let us take the leadEvery emotion, intense or light, are important to us, in one way or another
We can't just be logical cause logic and emotions actually need each other

Ignoring logic and just using emotions can be dangerous to human, and vice versa
The five elements to nature and emotion to humans are blessing by universe
Nature won't be complete without its five elements and so won't be humans without emotions
Emotions aren't dumb but a way to experience things and not just running same motions

Ashis Pahi

Ashis Pahi, pursuing Master degree in Commerce (Accounts), and regular writer in Your Quote platform since 2017. He loves to write poems, shayari, quotes, and spare my time in reading novels and try to learn different languages of his country. He strongly believe in himself. His determination is much more important than dedication.

Elements of this Universe:

Since the universe came into existence especially in the milky galaxy or we called it Akash Ganga in which we all surviving for the last millions and millions of years ago in this beautiful planet which has the sustainability of survival. This is the only planet where all the necessary and existing elements we get for survival as compared to other planets. We have Fire, Water, Air, Space. As other planets don't have.

Luckily, I'm here and enjoying this beautiful world by taking oxygen and releasing carbon dioxide into the atmosphere and that carbon dioxide is being used by the trees.

Fire is the important element which is used by all the people in this world forcooking food and to do ritual by the Brahmins on the occasions of Puja and festivals.

Space is such a place where all the stars, the whole unseen universe exists and now we humans have reached there to study further regarding the universe.

Water is the es sential and important element of each people living in this universe. Due to water lots of people gets to drink to erase their hunger and thirst. Many countries are there where water is becoming a challenge for survival.

We Must Keep All These Resources in A Safe Position and Hand Them Over to Our Next Generation to Enjoy The Way We Are Doing Right Now.

Priyanshi Mittal

Priyanshi, an enthusiastic writer who writes to pour her heart to the world to aspire it with her own experiences and feelings. Decorates her words with the depth of her heart and she believes that life is a journey with vivid twists and turns to be explored in every moment.
Ig I'd: _soul_ful_poetry_

धरती माँ

आज फिर मन किया माँ
तेरी भूमि पर तिरंगा लहराने का
इस पावन धरा से भ्रस्टाचार मिटाने का,
हर निर्दोष पर हुए जुल्म का हिसाब चुकाने का,
आज फिर मन किया माँ
तेरी मिट्टी को मेहकाने का,
वीरो की इस जन्म-भूमि पर
श्रध्दा सुमन चढाने का,
अंग्रेजी पढते बच्चों को,
देश प्रेम सिखलाने का,
नौजवानों के भीतर मातृ प्रेम जगाने का,
आज फिर मन किया माँ
तेरी धरती पे मिट जाने का
तुझपें सर्वस्व लुटाने का,
आज फिर मन किया माँ।

Vishal K R

Vishal.K.R , a 20 year old medical undergraduate from Bangalore , has been an avid book reader and a prolific writer. He has the credit of coauthoring various anthologies in several publications and had won 2nd prize in literary competition held on World Tuberculosis Day. History, philosophy, romance, mystery and adventure are his genre of interest. He likes to express his thoughts and views via literature, which leaves a profound impact on reader's mind. His thoughts and actions are unique and impressive. His pastime includes book reading and creative writing
Follow him on miraquill @krvishal
Follow him on Insta - enigma_6001.

Five Elements Exist in Our Life Too.

Water, to keep our thoughts like the fluid emotion, dynamic and never is stagnant. Life has to go on, else it breeds horrendous thoughts.

Air, to sustain us, not just us, but the blessings we receive, nature kissed pollen that floats around us. A lesson we learn, if the place you reside isn't for you, take the risk and embark, the fertile days will arrive soon, for you to blossom.

Fire, the one gives us light, and can scorch at the same time. We use it to guide our path, but can destroy us if we use it in the wrong way. Souls take up the flame to reach heaven, Jack o laterns fright the spirit with the same old fire.

Earth - children swallow earth, earth swallows the ones that have hopped the twig. Disease, famine and wars fought on the very soil we reside, why fight, when we aren't the permanent residents on the Earth.

Space - Fascinating life one needs to explore. Hides various mysteries, similar to our future. Never be a void, fill with virtues and set an example to others to embark on the same journey as yours. K ing may die, but he continues to reign in people's heart.

The 5 Elements in Nature

Helps our toxic thoughts to denature,
Fire to destroy our egos,
Earth to sustain my amigos
Air to help me think,
with surprise and make ego sing its swan song.
Space reminds me of void so long,
Life is but a mystery,
Continuous preaching to me by history,
A void filled by one's ownvirtues, to heaven he ascends, when interrogated, can affirm his engagements he undertook on Earth.
Water, to wash away doubts that arise in my mind.
Life mustn't be like inscriptions onsand, eroded by the roaring waves. But rather, like the inscriptions on stone walls, reflecting our views for millennium together.
Preaching even after one vanishes in thinair, swallowed by the Earth below, worms and vermin's consume the unholy garb , releasing the soul back to the paradise he belong.

T. Priyadharshini

She's Priyadharshini. Mommy's girl. The person she loves the most in her life is her mom. Pursued her masters in English literature. She was about to kickstart her PhD. She's a diehard disciple of Bruce Lee. A language lover she's. Certified in Japanese language. Her happiness is giving soul to her contemplations and inking it down. A budding writer and a movie lover too.

Tears of Earth

Normally a sapling takes years to transform into a healthy tree. But we humans are assassinating it within a fraction of seconds. Bracing greeny trees are replaced by sky high buildings. The underpinning of t hose buildings are not just bricks and stones, but the bruised scars of our mother earth. Still now, we are not letting those scars to heal, instead we are making it worser by whacking off the trees. Feeling wretched to sense that, we are living amongst such filthy aura. The earth is found with countless crevices. Our mother land's whimper is falling on our deaf ears. We have perished our own land, and now we are dying for water and oxygen. Five months of this year have passed, so far approximately 248 farmers were confirmed dead. They committed suicide due to insufficient irrigation, crop failure, drought, poverty and so on. They plenished us with contented food but, they are dying due to lack of food. Do they deserve this?! The bitter truth is that it's we, who ruined our mother earth. So, it's our sheer responsibility to lend our hands to the farmers. The tears of the earth can only be swabbed by the sweat of the farmers and only they can rejuvenate it's purity.

E-fface it's bruises.
A-ssauge it's pain.
R-evive it's freshness.
T-reasure it.
H-eal it.

Aditi Kumari

She is Aditi kumari. She doing her B.Sc. in biotechnology from St. Xavier college, Ranchi. she loves to write poems, quotes, write ups and stories She wrote her first poem in standard V. After that she is passionate for writings.

(1)

"Earth and sky, woods and fields, lakes and rivers, the mountains and the sea, are excellent schoolmates, and teach some of us more than we can learn from books."

- John Muir.

Everything in this world is made with natures elements. Nature teaches us how to be hard working and goal oriented like anearth, help others and be a healer like a water, be passionate and persistent towards our dreams like a fire, be gentle and calm like an air, be kind, understanding and comfortable home for beloved ones.
When you discover nature, what truly it is - you discover yourself. Nature is the best and most comfortable home you can ever had. A home in which you feel only love and care, discover your true self, the spiritual satisfaction.
The butterfly counts moment not months, and in that they feel enough time.
Those who are afraid, lonely or unhappy, the best remedy for them is to go outside, somewhere where they can be quiet, alone with the heavens, nature and god. When one is in the lap of nature, then he will feel that all is as it should be and that god wishes to see people happy, amidst the simple beauty of nature. Nature brings solace in all troubles.
Nature's peace will flow into us as sunshine flows into trees. the winds will blow their own freshness into us, and storms their energy, while love and cares will drop off like an autumn leaf.
Live in each season as it passes, breath the air, drink the drink, taste the fruit, play with butterflies, and resign yourself to the influence of the nature.

“Every Walk in With Nature, One Receives Far More Than He Seeks."

Navjot Singh

Navjot singh , an aspiring author and a physiotherapist has worked on multiple anthologies including Chimera and Vibgyor also projects including the famous Harry Potter fan fiction, "Harry Potter and The Curse of The Lying Prophecy." And 165-B Resident.
He loves to write about nature, love and self-worth.
Author can be reached on his Instagram
@the_vintage_soul
Email- nj970816@gmail.com

The Elements of Life

I always wondered how life was made,
Some say big bang and some believe in Oparin-Haldane,
The way life was created is not clear enough,
I don't think it was this smooth it definitely would have been so tough,
Another thing i noticed that our body is made of five elements,
Air, water, earth, fire and space all a given to us on rent,
On rent by our mother nature,
But role of these is very major,
Every elements plays different role,
All combine to make us one whole,
From air we breath from air we fly,
Only air can help make us sigh,
Its cools one when one feels hot,
May also sting on its own shot,
Water is all around us everytime,
Wasting it is considered as a wittfull crime,
Water can quench the thirsty,
But will cause terror if became bursty,
Fire is the most Versatile element of all,
It may be huge and it may be small,
Everyone loves the low eb and enjoys the heat,
But when Hephaestus roar even Boreas shivers and have to leave the seat,
Under control it maybe boon,
Can destroy life if insolent like a brune
From fire life starts and fire it ends,
Will you enjoy or get destroyed it depends,
Earth and space are underrated among them,
Not considered important but then run all realms,
Space we occupy will once go hollow,

But earth will be there to follow,
Follow the steps it always take,
Without even applying the break,
Even religious scripts says,
From five elements the human body is made,
We are clever enough to know this,
Our end will be becoming one with these elements,
But still we are foolish enough to feel proud of it.....

Maniska Das

She's an icy breeze to the firing sensation through her creative writing. Dominating silence over freaking loud crowd, depicting a lighted Brain and peaceful mentality. Inspired from the high school poem of Robert Frost, 'The Road Not Taken' she chose writing to be her passion, as the less travelled one in this busy world, which makes all the difference. As a young writer of 18, she believes that 'Everything can be expressed with a pen and paper while touching the sky the beyond your imagination.'

Belonging to the Holy Shri Jagannath Dham, Puri, Odisha, she has the purity in her sacred writings.

As writing is an art to be discovered, she hopes to get her imaginations explored.

Earth

The earth lies in a physical body,
Where we live, what we are,
Hold on to something and stop the one,
Hearing birds chirping around,
Smelling the petrichor's divinity,
To tasting the purity of ambrosia,
Touching the serenity of nature

Space

I found you in the bodies of space,
That's what the distance between us;
I couldn't see you beyond the light of stars;
Probably that's why you're so far!
Still, I admire you all the milky way,
Maybe it symbolizes the strong connection within,
Space's nonresistance teaches us to live mutually,
Avoiding millions of distractions; smiling perpetually.

Water

Flexible to be in any container,
Teaching us to open the mind,
It's calm and coldness soothes the soul,
Its absence takes the lives away,
It can be seen; it can be felt,
But no odour it has,
Hearing the sound of raindrop I went,
Tasted the heaven's gift it was!

Fire

Rising a bit of temperature every minute,
I wonder to burn my guilt in fire,
But failed to give my regretting wax,
As even candles melt touching fire,
It doesn't mean I'm weak enough,
It doesn't mean I'll rebuff,
The ashes said it's done Afterall,
It purified my heart and soul.

Air

Unstable movement in any direction,
Just like the man's unconscious mind,
Not knowing the route where to go,
Started a journey from unnamed road,
Suddenly I got goosebumps,
And a blow of wind marked the road,
I knew where to reach now;
Till infinity above and in everything beyond.

Mohanapriya.K

Mohanapriya.K is a budding writer from Tamilnadu, India. She has completed her Bachelor's degree in Engineering stream. She has been a writer for one year as her passion. She wants to be a best compiler and voice over artist in future. She has been co -author of 210 anthologies so far and worked in many record holding, internationally published anthologies and magazines. She participated in many writing contests on instagram and received certificates. Yet she sincerely hope that this writing journey of her will continue as sweetly as it is now and will bring her many successes. You can find her writings on her instagram page.

Instagram: @colours_honey_official
E-mail : doraa.kutty@gmail.com

About Water

We need to save water.

We need to have water available to our next generation just as we have access to water without famine.

It is important to store water without wasting it.
It is necessary for everyone to get down in an effort to do so.

The government should also make some efforts for that.

People need to realize the importance of this.

Only with some of the government's efforts will people understand its seriousness.

We need to think not only about this generation but also about the next generation.

Save that rainwater without wasting it when it rains.
The lakes and ponds around us need to be drained fr equently without getting dirty.

Lakes and ponds should not be used as dumping grounds.

We must realize that it is bad for us if we use it that way.

Water is an important factor in producing current.

Importance Of Water

Holy river - Ganga plays a very important role in the myths we hear and read.

Mata Ganga and Bishmar, the son of Ganga's mother, play a very important role in the great epic Mahabharata.

Ganga river is a holy place where the elderly is expected to spend the last days of their lives with happy devotion.

This is one of the most important places in India.

It seems that such a place should have been blessed by all of us Indians in India.

It is home to a large number of gods, sages and agoraphobes.

But the river Ganga is said to be more polluted now than ever before.

The Indian government must take the right steps to clean it up as before.

So, if we do not store water, if there is notenough water in this world, then we all have to suffer.

Water is essential not only for humans but also for animals and birds.

Husaina S

Husaina S is a Mediocre student from Nagercoil,Kanniyakumari,India.Eventhough she is from a strict Islamic background, she tries to expose her ideas and skills through her writing. Her aim is to become a great poet and writer. Also, she works in NGOs to protect humanity and Earth! She is also Editor, Compiler, and Co -Author for Many anthologies and Magazines. To Contact her, you can just search husaina_25 in Instagram

Her mail id: husainahuss000@gmail.com

(1)

My Dear Human Beings,
I'm EARTH! Do You remember Me?
Once I was Full of Trees
And gave you Energies...
But What you did?
Cut it down! Constructed Roads!
Drived Vehicles on Me!
And made Me Polluted!
But still I loved You...
And Cared You...
But again!
You Threwed Plastics on Me!
Made Me Nasty!
So! "I" and My Friend "Nature"
Decided to give You a Gift
Named "CORONA"
To Take REVENGE!!!

Adhyatm Singh

Adhyatm Singh,
He is living in delhi,
Doing his graduation in Indira Kala Sangit Vishwavidyalaya (Public university in Khairagarh, Chhattisgarh)
And doing his grades in piano (Trinity College London), India.
He loves to write poetry and songs & he is a voracious reader.

(1)

The air serves me with her head,
And light wraps me in total & absolute earth;
I inhale air, and space swallowing me in wrath.
The flux, The Flux; though matter; unchanging.
Do you hearing the waterly poems of earth.
Yeah, it is there, there; leaves floating on me.
The unknown nebula, the galaxies; I am of it's tribe.
Stars; rooms of wrath, monstrous suns & phatomic-moons.
Leave, O'Leave, Leave those tedious nights or accept,
Let me hide my thoughts on earth, let me reveal the truth;
In the ear of ancient air of inferno's garden.
I do not know what is it; the fire which burns the time.
To be in any form; that is the motive, don't be here & there.
Lets conquer the earth; for non-conformity goes to eternity.
Mystical, before we were born, all forces have been
delighted.
Now,in this endless plot, I stand with my all elemental rocks..

(2)

We live on the edge of fire,
In the inferno of the earth,
Our greatest desire; air & light.
Let us move; on earth, on water.
For every element is made unto death.
It is human, that is alien to himself,
They don't realize that they are
made of undying elements, born to fly,
Let's sink in water, touch the air,
Lay on earth, bring the fire unto space.
Children's, interpret the ocean, they
Sees as air evolves thru the sea.
Now; realize, the thing in the air
that never changes, though the bodies
Change; but elements remain the same.
Air, fire, water, earth, space; lives in us.

Poojalakshmi. V

Poojalakshmi is a young budding author from Tamilnadu. Currently she is pursuing her Masters in English. She has a great interest in writing stories, quotes, poems etc.So far, she has been co-author of more than 20 anthologies.

It's Me - The Water

Sometimes I'm white
Sometimes I'm blue
Sometimes I'm green
Name my place
But everywhere I am
I visit every year
With my charming smile
From the dark black clouds
To improvise the growth
Of every flora and fauna
I love coming here
Everyone says I'm their life saver
But I don't think so- There
Are much more than me
I am a free bird you see
I flow flawlessly through
These groovy hills, local farms
None to stop me
Finally, I seep into the ground
To enrich the soil- However
These humans find a way
To get me though
They have me in abundance
Some places I wish to visit
Where people strive for me
I promise I'll get to you
That's my ultimate purpose.

Rupsha Mitra

Rupsha Mitra is from Kolkata. She is in college. Writing is her passion. She finds a way to communicate her thoughts through her poetry and short stories. Her insta handle is @__rupshaaaa__

Lesson

"I did not understand what you said. Are they some scary creatures?" she asked.
"They are not scary, my child. They cannot be. They are the reason of your existence." He said. She looked at Him with her little eyes. He talked about fascinating tales but the little unborn mind could not gobble it.
"What do they signify? Am I here for them?" she asked.
"Certainly, my child." He replied with calm eyes. Her little eyes had a spark that could lit up any human's heart.
"Do you see it?" He said pointing at the farthest corner. It appeared small from the distance.
"It rotates. Is that where I will go?" she asked.
He laughed at her sweetness. "Yes. That is Mother Earth. That is your home. Do you know what does Mother Earth say?"
"What does it say? Tell me. I want to know."
"It says stability. It means firmness or the strength to endure."
"What about the scariest one? And tell me about that magic. It passed by me but I did not see it."
He gave out a little laugh again. After putting a hand on her delicate head, He said, "Fire and Wind, little soul. They are not scary. They too h ave a message for you. Fire says power and wisdom. It comes from within your soul. They drive you to the right path of your life. Wind whispers compassion. It is about pity and concern about other's sufferings. You know, you will be happy once you try to make others happy"
"I know about the fifth one. It is…"
He laughed and said, "Space. It is knowledge. It is like the space above you. It has got no limits and you can gain as much as you want."
"Will they come with me?"

"They are within you. Your deeds will represent them, don't worry. Now it is time my child. Time to step on the earth. You are going to come out of your mother's womb soon."

Flairs and Glairs, a platform by a student for the students. We are esteemed youth struggling to carve out our path for our future and we follow a basic mindset Since everyone is not born with allround skills. Joining hands with people who are born to execute it with perfection is the best way to evol ve. Self-Evolution is the need of the hour but, evolving as a community is what we strive for. The initiative as kickstarted by, Founder - Mr. Shubham Shah with the motive to utilize the skillset and talent of writing has now a team of 10+ people who are actively participating into newer forms of learning and discovering talents among youngsters. We Provide platform and services like Publishing opportunities, Open mics, Workshops, Hands-on training. Operating with Brand Name of Flairs and Glairs (Publication House), we offer the chance of elevating a passionate writer to an esteemed author With Brand name Teekhe Zasbaaat. We bring to you an opportunity to get accustomed with the Public Speaking and Presenting of Thoughts along with regular challen ges to brush up your inking spirit. The newest initiative to extend our services we introduced in a new writing Platform- The Glittering Fables and Ink Over Tears.

We Choose to Fly Like A Falcon than to be

a Leg Pulling Crab.

www.ingramcontent.com/pod-product-compliance
Ingram Content Group UK Ltd.
Pitfield, Milton Keynes, MK11 3LW, UK
UKHW022005190726
13853UKWH00004B/1751